FANTORIA

PUBLISHING & ENTERTAINMENT

Presents

Executive Producer

(AKA DEDICATED TO)
DaVINCI ALEXANDER SIRLS (MY SON)

Story Art

JQ SIRLS

Starring

LITTLE BOY & FAMILY
THE MOON

Casting

JQ'S IMAGINATION

Animation

NO ONE. IT'S A PICTURE BOOK.

THE ART IN THIS BOOK WAS CREATED IN SOFT TRIBUTE
TO 1920S – 1960S COMIC BOOKS AND ANIMATION.

FIRST EDITION. ISBN: 978-0-578-57888-0. LIBRARY OF CONGRESS CONTROL NUMBER: 2019914686. MANUFACTURED IN CHINA.

FANTORIA (WORLD OF FANTORIA, LLC) 138 N BRAND BLVD STE 200 UNIT 161, GLENDALE, CA 91203-4617

SPECIAL THANKS: LAI THING SHENG, AMY SKLANSKY & LATOYA EBONY SIRLS

The MOON Is Following ME!

JQ SIRLS

FANTORIA

I THINK...

I TRIED TO TELL MY DAD, BUT HE DIDN'T BELIEVE ME. HE JUST LAUGHED AND ASKED,

"WHY WOULD THE MOON FOLLOW YOU?"

I THOUGHT ABOUT IT.

WHAT IF THE MOON IS MADE OF CHEESE!? IT'S THE QUEEN OF CHEESE!

SHE'S MAD AT ME FOR EATING SEVEN CHEESE SANDWICHES LAST WEEK.

WHICH MEANS THAT SHE'S FOLLOWING ME TO MAKE SURE I DON'T EAT ANY MORE OF HER CHEESY CHILDREN!

I TRIED TO TELL MY MOM, BUT SHE DIDN'T BELIEVE ME. SHE JUST LAUGHED AND SAID,

"THE MOON IS NOT A QUEEN MADE OF CHEESE, AND LOTS OF KIDS EAT CHEESE SANDWICHES. WHY WOULD THE MOON FOLLOW YOU?"

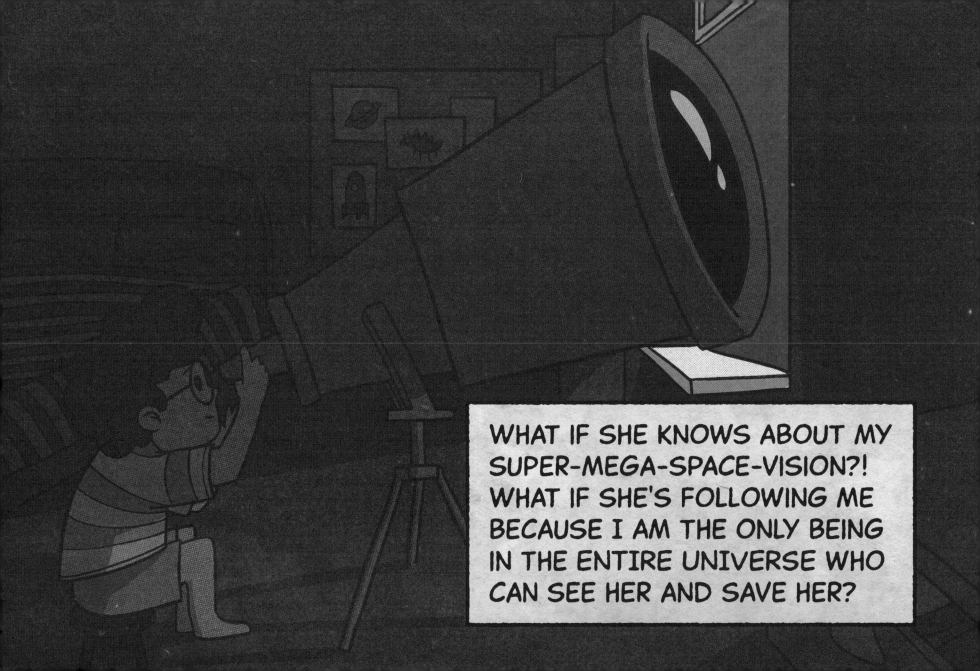

THAT WOULD MEAN THAT I AM A

TEN-LEGGED
ALIEN
SPACE COW
HERO

I TRIED TO TELL MY BIG BROTHER, BUT
HE DIDN'T BELIEVE ME. HE JUST LAUGHED
AND SAID,

"THERE IS NO SUCH THING AS A TEN-LEGGED
ALIEN SPACE COW, AND THERE ARE LOTS
OF KIDS WITH TELESCOPES. THE MOON IS
NOT FOLLOWING YOU."

I THINK...

THE MOON IS A

SUPERHERO

SAVING ME FROM THE WOOGLY MONSTERS IN THE DARK!

I HAVE MY VERY OWN SUPERHERO.

The End

And That's All!